For Daniel
—*J.S.*

For Chris and Sal's new baby
—*J.C.*

tiger tales
an imprint of ME Media, LLC
202 Old Ridgefield Road
Wilton, CT 06897
First published in the United States 2002
Originally published in Great Britain 2002
by Little Tiger Press, London
Text © 2002 Julie Sykes
Illustrations © 2002 Jane Chapman
CIP data available
ISBN 1-58925-015-X
First US Edition
Printed in Belgium
1 3 5 7 9 10 8 6 4 2

DORA'S CHICKS

by Julie Sykes   *Illustrated by* Jane Chapman

tiger tales

One morning, Dora opened her eyes. Her six
fluffy chicks were beginning to stir.

"My chicks will be hungry," clucked Dora.
"I'd better go and look for their breakfast."

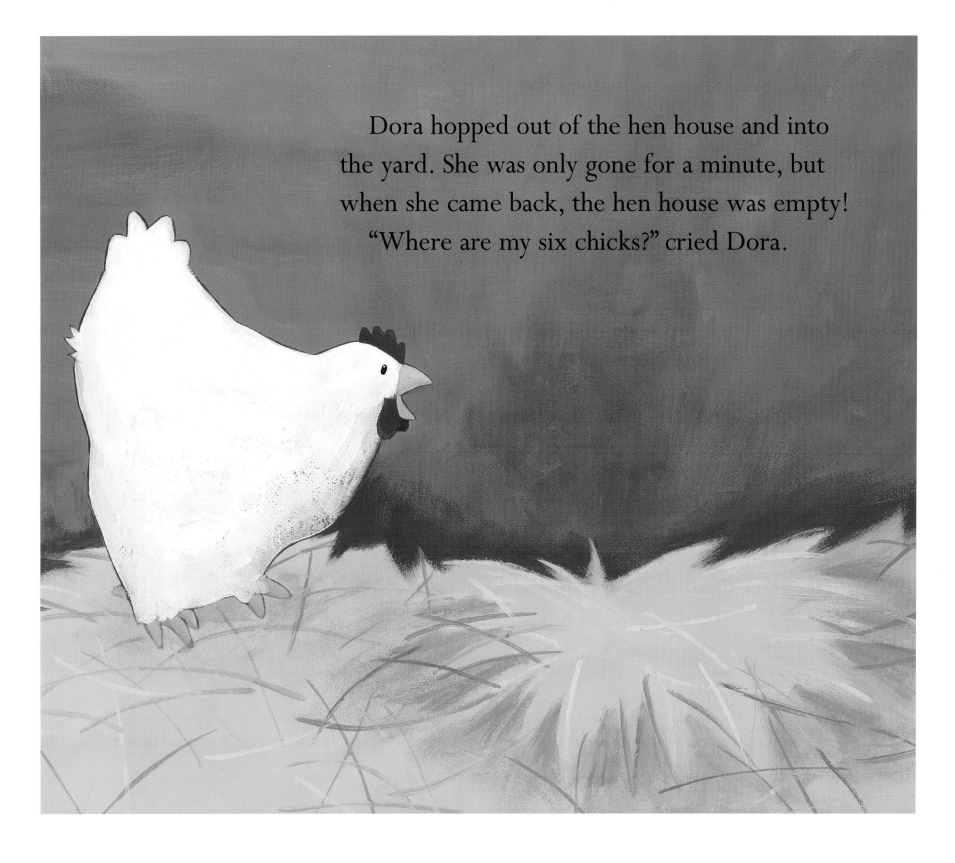

Dora hopped out of the hen house and into the yard. She was only gone for a minute, but when she came back, the hen house was empty! "Where are my six chicks?" cried Dora.

Quickly, Dora ran back into the barnyard and over to the pigpen.

"Hello, Penny," she called. "I've lost my chicks. Have you seen them?"

"Sorry, Dora, I'm feeding my piglets," oinked Penny. "I haven't noticed where your chicks have gone."

Dora watched the piglets rushing
toward their mother. But who was
that following them?

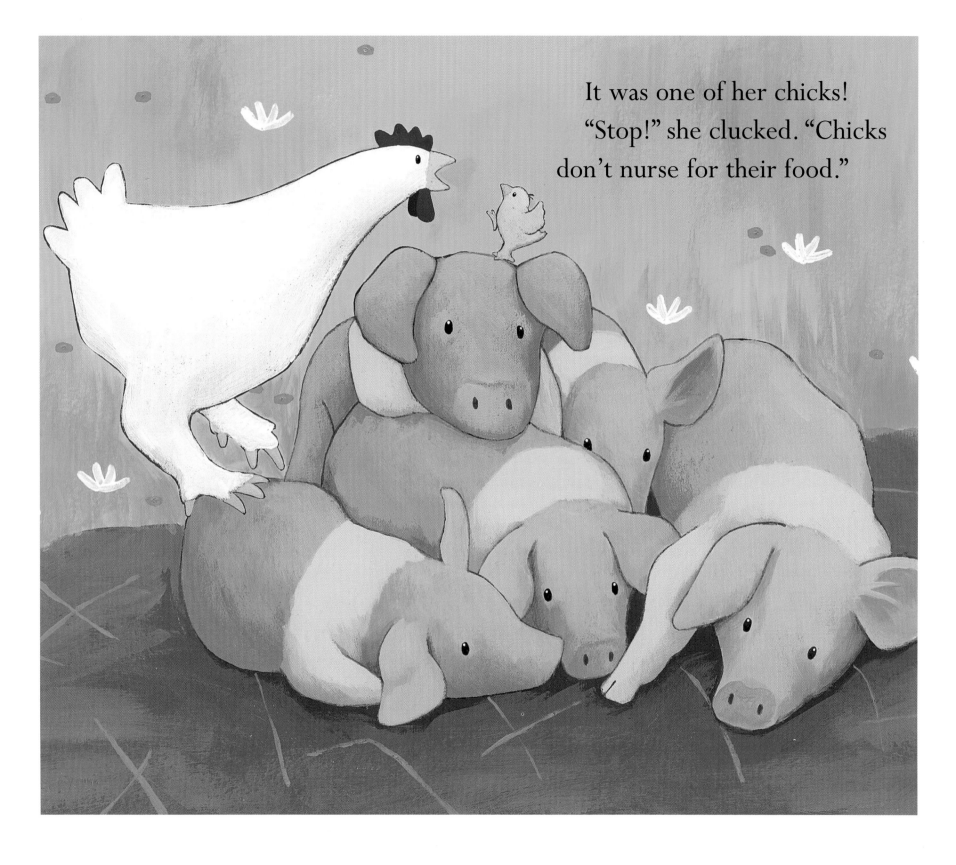

It was one of her chicks!
"Stop!" she clucked. "Chicks
don't nurse for their food."

Dora hopped after her chick and
rescued it before it got trampled.
"One chick safe," said Dora,
feeling a little happier. "But that
leaves five to find."

Dora and her one chick went down to the pond.
Debbie Duck was there, getting her ducklings into line.

"Hello, Debbie," called Dora. "I've lost some chicks.
Have you seen them?"

"I'm teaching my ducklings to fish for their food,"
quacked Debbie. "So I haven't seen where your chicks
have gone."

Dora watched the ducklings splash into the
water. The last one couldn't keep up. Suddenly,
Dora realized it wasn't a duckling at all!

It was another of her chicks!
"Wait!" cried Dora. "Chicks don't
fish for food. They can't swim!"

Dora chased after her chick, and stopped it from jumping into the water just in the nick of time.

"Two chicks safe," said Dora, feeling quite pleased. "But that leaves four to find."

Dora continued on her search. On the way past the big barn she stopped to look inside. Honey Horse was showing her foal how to eat hay.

"Hello, Honey," called Dora. "I've lost some chicks. Have you seen them?"

"Sorry, Dora, but I've been so busy with my foal, I haven't noticed your chicks," neighed Honey.

Sadly, Dora hopped back
toward the door. But who was
that climbing those bales of hay?

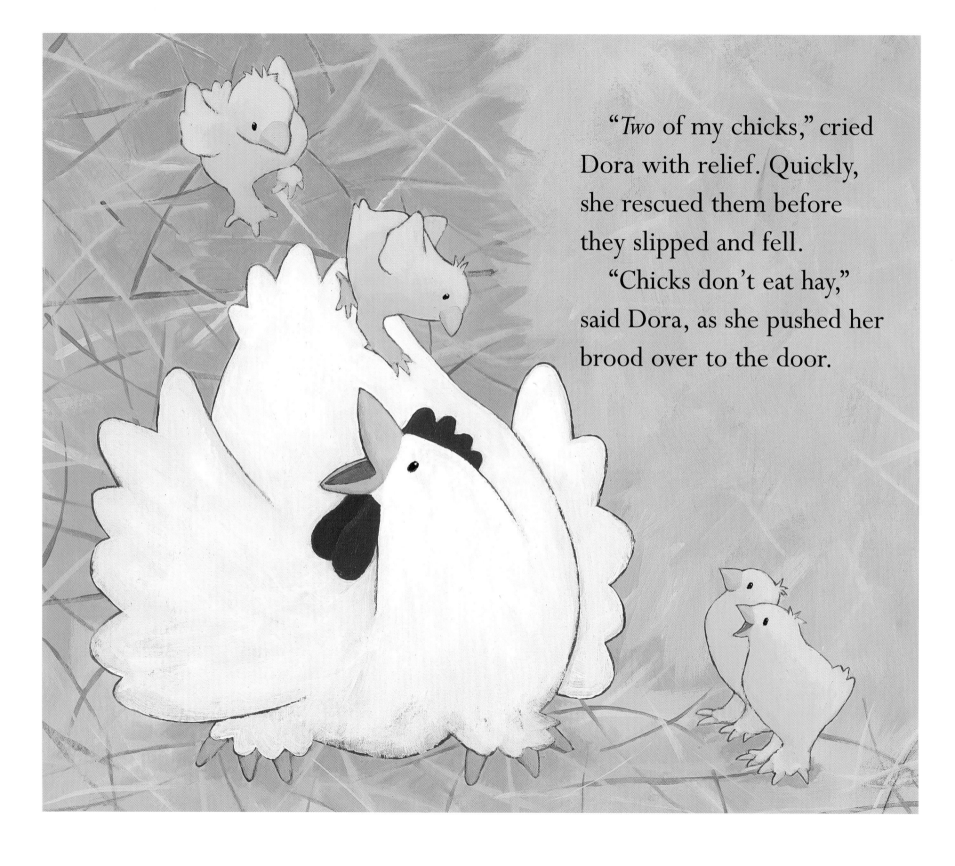

"*Two* of my chicks," cried Dora with relief. Quickly, she rescued them before they slipped and fell.

"Chicks don't eat hay," said Dora, as she pushed her brood over to the door.

Back in the sunlight, Dora counted her chicks.

"One, two, three, four. But I have six chicks, so there are still two missing."

Dora searched everywhere for her last two chicks.
She searched in the yard, and she searched in the
orchard. She squeezed under the gate and . . .

saw Bobby Bird on the other side of the road, pulling up worms to eat.

"Cheep, cheep, cheep," cried Dora's chicks, feeling hungry. "We want breakfast!"

Dora was just about to turn back, when she saw . . .

her fifth chick crossing the road
to reach Bobby and his worms.
    "Don't move!" ordered Dora.
"You must *never* cross a road
without looking both ways first.
You might get hurt."

Bobby flew over to see
what all the fuss was about.
"Goodness, what a lot
of chicks," he exclaimed.
"Yes," said Dora. "But
I have six chicks, so one is
still missing."

Dora and her chicks hopped through
the upper field. They flapped across
the lower field.

They passed the cowshed and the doghouse. And all the time, Dora kept looking for her sixth chick.

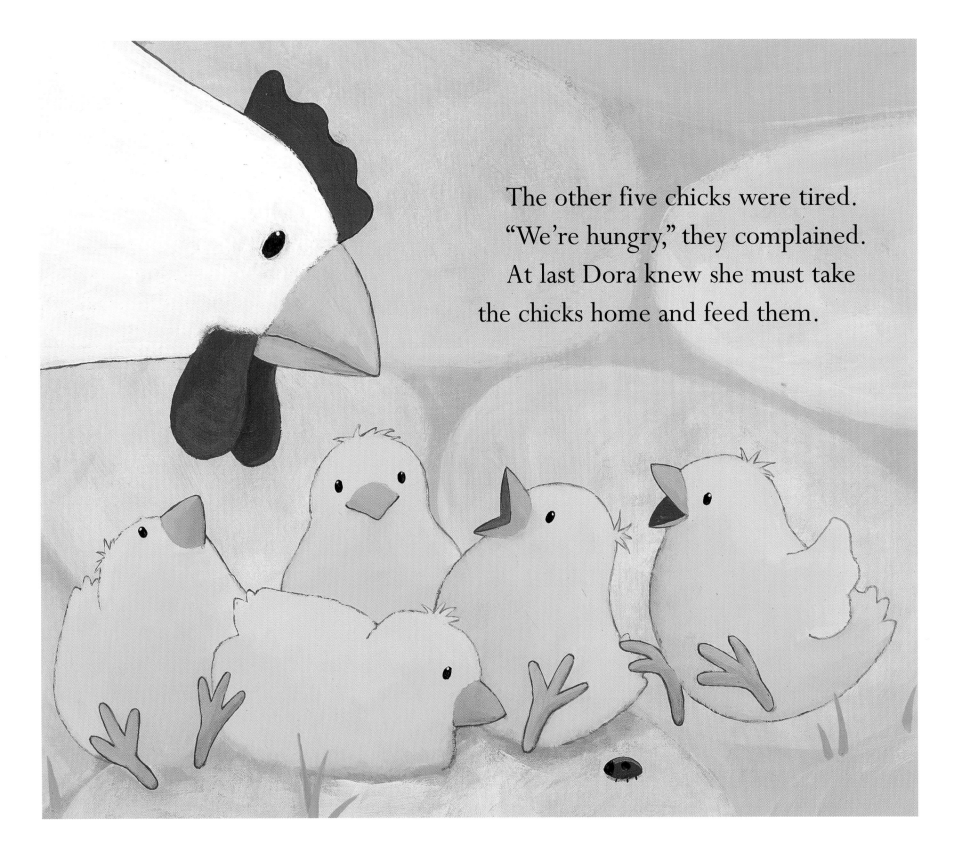

The other five chicks were tired. "We're hungry," they complained. At last Dora knew she must take the chicks home and feed them.

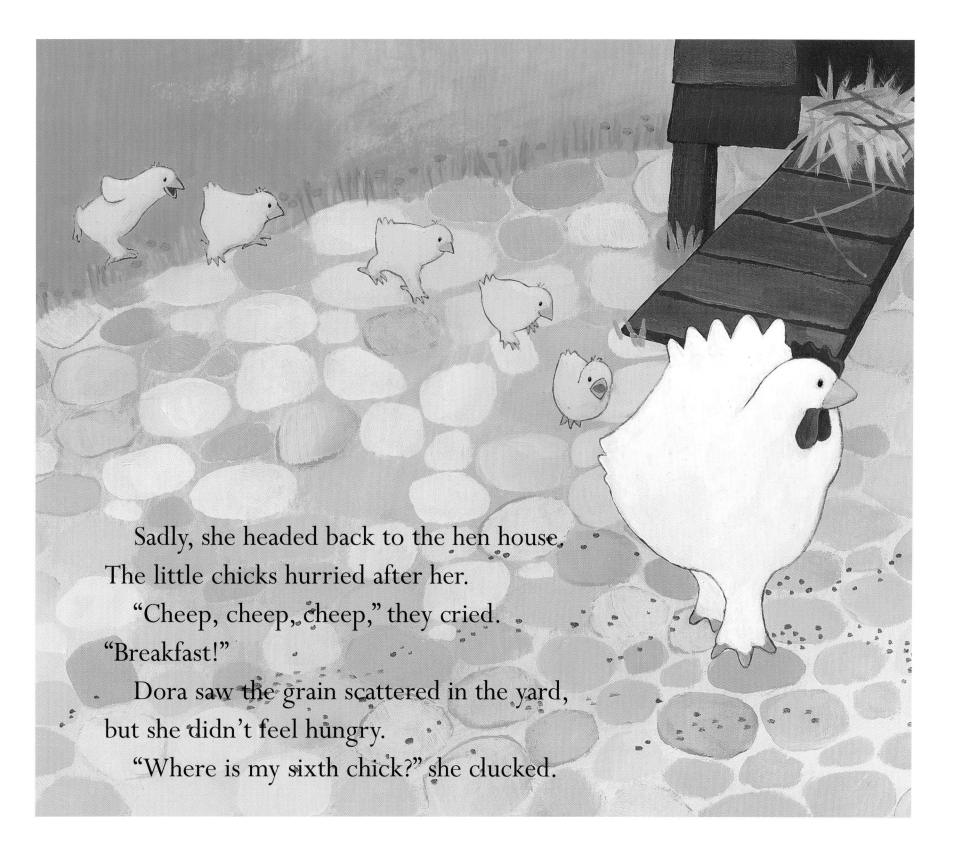

Sadly, she headed back to the hen house.
The little chicks hurried after her.

"Cheep, cheep, cheep," they cried.
"Breakfast!"

Dora saw the grain scattered in the yard,
but she didn't feel hungry.

"Where is my sixth chick?" she clucked.

"Here I am!" chirped a tiny voice. Dora's sixth chick was already back in the yard, pecking for breakfast! Dora clucked with joy. At last all her chicks were home again.

"Excuse me, Dora, can you help me?
I need to find some moss for my nest."
It was Bobby Bird.
"We'll help you, Bobby," said Dora,
"as soon as the chicks are finished
with breakfast!"